To my wonderful mom
—S.H.

For Kate
Love, Auntie Jane x
—J.M.

NANCY PAULSEN BOOKS
an imprint of Penguin Random House LLC
375 Hudson Street
New York, NY 10014

Library of Congress Cataloging-in-Publication Data
Names: Haft, Sheryl, author. | Massey, Jane, 1967– illustrator.
Title: Baby Boo, I love you / Sheryl Haft ; illustrated by Jane Massey.
Description: New York, NY : Nancy Paulsen Books, 2017.
Summary: "A little girl takes care of her beloved baby doll"—Provided by publisher.
Identifiers: LCCN 2016022384 | ISBN 9780399547829 (hardback)
Subjects: | CYAC: Stories in rhyme—Fiction. | Dolls—Fiction. | BISAC: JUVENILE FICTION / Family / General (see also headings
under Social Issues). | JUVENILE FICTION / Toys, Dolls, Puppets. | JUVENILE FICTION / Imagination & Play.
Classification: LCC PZ8.3.H1185 Bab 2017 | DDC [E]—dc23
LC record available at https://lccn.loc.gov/2016022384.

Manufactured in China by RR Donnelley Asia Printing Solutions Ltd.
ISBN 9780399547829
10 9 8 7 6 5 4 3 2 1

Design by Annie Ericsson.
Text set in Tuff Normal.
The art for this book was created using gouache, pencil crayon, watercolor, india ink, and collage.

Baby-Boo, I LOVE YOU

Sheryl Haft

illustrated by
Jane Massey

 NANCY PAULSEN BOOKS

When it is morning,
what will I bring?

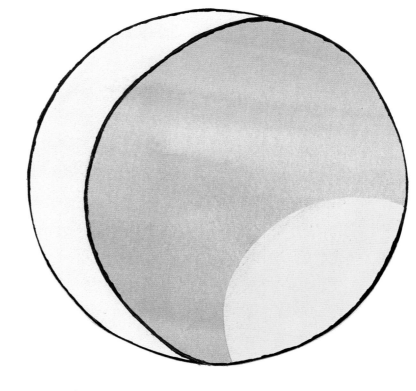

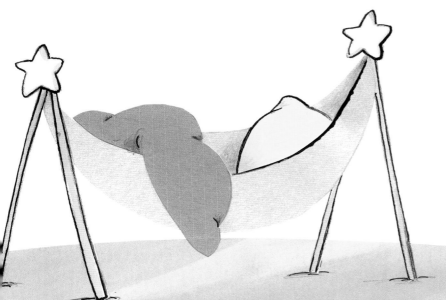

A kiss for you
and a song to sing.

When you are hiding,
what will I do?

I'll find you, baby.
Peekaboo!

Me and you.
One and two.

Wherever we go,
whatever we do,

Baby-Boo,

I love you.

What if you're scared
to slide and climb?

I'll catch you, baby.
Every time.

What if you're hungry
for cookies and tea?

I'll put out a picnic
for you and for me.

I'll pick you a dandelion,
blow you a wish.

Then rub-a-dub, baby,
splash-a-dee-splish!

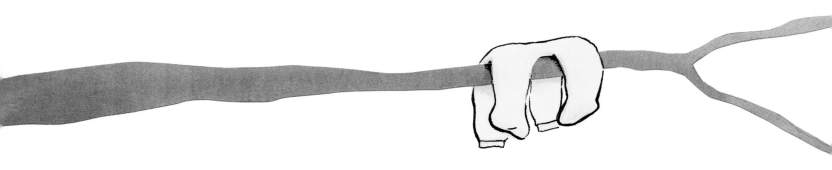

Me and you.
One and two.

Wherever we go,
whatever we do,

Baby-Boo,
I love you.

What if the wind blows
and up comes a storm?

I'll hug you real tight
and keep you so warm.

What if the rain comes,

plippity-plop?

Don't worry, baby.
You won't feel a drop!

Whatever we do,
I'll be there for you.

Over a rainbow
and all the world through.

Baby-Boo,

I love you.